The Firebird in Russian folklore is a fiery, illuminated bird; magical, iconic, coveted. Its feathers continue to glow when removed, and a single feather, it is said, can light up a room. Some who claim to have seen the Firebird say it even has glowing eyes. The Firebird is often the object of a quest. In one famous tale, the Firebird needs to be captured to prevent it from stealing the king's golden apples, a fruit bestowing youth and strength on those who partake of the fruit. But in other stories, the Firebird has another mission: it is always flying over the earth providing hope to any who may need it. In modern times and in the West, the Firebird has become part of world culture. In Igor Stravinsky's ballet *The Firebird,* it is a creature half-woman and half-bird, and the ballerina's role is considered by many to be the most demanding in the history of ballet.

The Overlook Press in the U.S. and Gerald Duckworth in the UK, in adopting the Firebird as the logo for its expanding Ardis publishing program, consider that this magical, glowing creature—in legend come to Russia from a faraway land—will play a role in bringing Russia and its literature closer to readers everywhere.

The Crocodile

Fyodor Dostoevsky

An Extraordinary Event, or a Show in the Arcade, The
True Story of How a Certain Gentleman of Familiar Age
and Familiar Appearance was Swallowed Alive by the
Arcade Crocodile, Completely, and Utterly, and What
Came Out.

Translated from the Russian by

S. D. Cioran

ARDIS PUBLISHERS
NEW YORK, NY

This edition published in the United States and the United Kingdom in
2013 by Ardis Publishers, an imprint of Peter Mayer Publishers, Inc.

NEW YORK:
The Overlook Press
Peter Mayer Publishers, Inc.
141 Wooster Street
New York, NY 10012
www.overlookpress.com
For bulk and special sales, please contact sales@overlookny.com

LONDON:
Gerald Duckworth Publishers Ltd.
90-93 Cowcross Street
London EC1M 6BF
www.ducknet.co.uk
info@duckworth-publishers.co.uk

Library of Congress Cataloging-in-Publication Data
Dostoevsky, Fyodor, 1821-1881.
The Crocodile, an extraordinary event.
Translation of: Krokodil.
I. Cioran, Samuel D. (Samuel David), 1941-   II. Title.
PG3326.K6   1984   891.73'3   84-20383

Printed in the United States of America
ISBN 978-1-4683-0154-0

2 4 6 8 10 9 7 5 3 1

Go to **www.ardisbooks.com** to read or
download the latest Ardis catalog.

CONTENTS

INTRODUCTION

In December of 1859 Dostoevsky was given permission
to return to St. Petersburg. Ten years of imprisonment
and Siberian exile were behind him as he set out to
refashion his literary career in the Russian capital. The
times were markedly different. Tsar Alexander II, who
had ascended the throne in 1855, had announced wide-
sweeping reforms: the emancipation of the serfs (sched-
uled for 1861); the reorganization of the army, judiciary
and government. On the literary front, journals and
newspapers enjoyed greater freedom to indulge in polemics.

Dostoevsky had long nurtured a desire to become
involved in some commercial literary enterprise. Together with his brother, Mikhail, he obtained the necessary permission in January of 1861 to begin publication
of a literary monthly entitled *Time* (*Vremya*). Mikhail
was named editor and financial manager for the journal

because Dostoevsky, owing to his political past, could not hold such a post. But Dostoevsky was the *de facto* editor and driving force behind the journal.

The years 1861-1865 were, by turns, stimulating, depressing and exhausting for Dostoevsky. In the midst of trying to reenter the mainstream of Russian literary life, Dostoevsky was buffeted by one loss after the other: the death of his wife, Mariya Dmitrievna, after a long bout of tuberculosis (April, 1864); the death of his brother, Mikhail (July, 1865); the forced closure by the authorities of *Time* (April, 1863); the collapse of *Epoch* (*Epokha*), the debt-ridden sequel to *Time* (June, 1865). These major losses unravelled against a wider backdrop that included Dostoevsky's sexually perverse and destructive relationship with his "mistress", Apollinariya Suslova (1862-63); his sexually unambiguous and short-lived relationship with Martha Brown (winter of 1864-65) and his hapless courtship of the young, attractive and intellectual Anna Korvin-Krukovskaya (1865). His attempts to keep his journalistic enterprises financially healthy generally represented a losing battle for Dostoevsky. He was constantly in debt, borrowing more money and trying to escape from his creditors.

A great deal of Dostoevsky's literary energies during this period were devoured by journalism and management. But despite the physically debilitating landscape of death, debt and "depravity", Dostoevsky nevertheless found the time to create the literary works which propelled him indisputably back into the front ranks of

Russian literature once more: *The Insulted and Injured* (1861); *Notes from the House of the Dead* (1862); *Notes from the Underground* (1864-65).

In the 1860's Russian literature in general and Russian journals in particular were expected to profess some ideological orientation. Obviously, the question of Russia's past, present and future loomed most largely in these discussions as rival groups adopted varying stances on Westernism versus Slavophilism, progressivism versus traditionalism, liberalism versus conservatism, materialism versus idealism. *Professions de foi* were mandatory for all serious journals and newspapers. Both of Dostoevsky's journals were prompt in making their ideological appeals to the reading public. Although Dostoevsky took pains to excoriate the various excesses of Slavophilism, nevertheless, it was probably natural for readers to identify him more closely with that particular camp. Above all, Dostoevsky gave his fervent support to a Russian nationalism that was both metaphysical and mystical. The symbol of Dostoevsky's allegiance to Russia was broadly encompassed in the term "soil" (*pochva*), and its adherents were "people of the soil" (*pochvenniki*). Russian soil was the repository for all the traditions, values and virtues that the author espied in Russia's past and present and which promised so much for the future. Although Dostoevsky had a (grudging?) respect for European culture and civilization and although he was willing to admit that Russia had benefitted from her association with Europe, nevertheless he felt that Russia was inherently superior and was now at the parting of ways with its stepmother to the West and about to embark on a new path that was uniquely Russian. The publicist and prophet in Dostoevsky often led him to proclaim exaggerated qualities for his countrymen: Russians were not boastful; they welcomed self-criticism; they spoke all languages; they were more "international" and "pan-human" than any other nation; they were the most adaptable people on earth; all classes in Russian society would merge into a single homogeneous mass because there was no inherent differences between educated Russians and the serfs; Pushkin was a universal poet without equal in world literature and none but the Russians could appreciate his profound talents.

Threatening this grandiloquent vision of Russia and Russians, however, were the malignant spread and blind acceptance of European ideas. By some sleight of hand Dostoevsky managed to create a single unappetizing salad of all the disparate and unwelcome European -ism's (liberalism, progressivism, utilitarianism, scientific determinism, materialism, etc.) under the catch-all title of "nihilism" and flavor it with a generous dressing of xenophobia whose recipe was concocted during his visits to Western Europe. Three minor works from this period of journalistic activity concentrated on his dislike of Europe and "nihilism": "A Nasty Tale" (1862), "Winter Notes on Summer Impressions" (1863), and "The Crocodile" (1865).

When viewed within the context of his polemics with the so-called "democratic press" in the early 1860's, "The Crocodile" merits particular attention. It is worth pointing out that Dostoevsky did not make the "democratic press" (Chernyshevsky and Saltykov-Shchedrin on *The Contemporary* [*Sovremennik*], or D. I. Pisarev and V. A. Zaitsev on *The Russian Word* [*Russkoe slovo*]) the sole targets for his wit and sarcasm, but, with admirable fairness, treated the liberal and conservative press to his barbs as well. The inspiration for "The Crocodile" allegedly stemmed from the happy coincidence of a true event (a German was exhibiting a crocodile in the capital in 1864) and the author's professed desire to write a fantastic tale in imitation of Gogol's novella, "The Nose". At the same time, however, Dostoevsky used the occasion to square off against various opponents. As a result, "The Crocodile" presents the reader with a patchwork quilt wherein the author has woven a fantastic plot and embroidered it with a lampoon directed against the Russian press, radical ideological trends and europeanization.

One of the leaders of Russian radicalism, Nikolai Gavrilovich Chernyshevsky (1828-89), figures very prominently in the literary history of "The Crocodile". Many critics at the time of the publication of "The Crocodile", as, indeed, is the case even today, believed that Dostoevsky had written a vicious and cowardly lampoon on Chernyshevsky. The latter was perhaps the most influential critic and positivist thinker in the late 1850's and early 1860's. His doctoral thesis, *The Aesthetic Relations of Art to Reality*, became a standard work for the radicals. Its basic tenet was that art was merely an imperfect imitation of reality and literature's function was to promote social change. Chernyshevsky's activities grew more radical after the Emancipation in 1861 as he was apparently chosen by the radical younger generation as their leader. One of the chief activities of this radical youth was the printing of proclamations that called for immediate and violent change. In 1862 Chernyshevsky was arrested on vague charges and imprisoned in the Petropavlovsk Fortress in St. Petersburg. It was during his confinement there that he wrote his most famous work, the social utopian novel, *What Is To Be Done?*. This novel, while admittedly lacking from a literary point-of-view, was a novel of social and revolutionary emancipation that had enormous appeal for the young radicals. In the various characters in the novel one encounters, almost for the first time in nineteenth century Russian literature, "positive" heroes who have a revolutionary vision of the future and provide exemplars of action with their own deeds and thoughts. The reader is introduced to Vera Pavlovna who not only is one of the first feminists in Russian literature, but who dreams the dream of some future ideal society where reason, science and social conscience reign supreme. And there is the young nobleman, Rakhmetov, who champions rationalism and self-discipline in the name of their great revolutionary cause. After a two-year imprisonment in the Petropavlovsk Fortress, Chernyshevsky was sentenced to penal servitude and exile in Siberia and Astrakhan. This sentence lasted more than twenty years before he was finally allowed to return to his native Saratov where he died in 1889.

If, indeed, Dostoevsky had intended a lampoon on Chernyshevsky then it would have seemed a very vile act inasmuch as Chernyshevsky had been sent to penal servitude in Siberia only the year before the appearance of "The Crocodile". Although later (and only much later) Dostoevsky claimed that such charges were utterly unfounded, the evidence is certainly suggestive. Chernyshevsky's ideas were extremely alien to Dostoevsky and Chernyshevsky was the avowed leader of the radical left that Dostoevsky despised so vehemently. Certainly, Dostoevsky could not have appreciated or liked the novel *What Is To Be Done?* since it clearly represented the most radical thoughts of Chernyshevsky on social change and upheaval. If one reads carefully Dostoevsky's account of the affair in *Diary of a Writer* (which is contained in the appendix to this translation), Dostoevsky does seem to damn Chernyshevsky with faint and ambiguous praise. And certainly, even as Dostoevsky admits despite himself, the allegory is vile but viable: Ivan Matveich, progressive, presumptuous and courting obvious danger, ends up in the belly of the crocodile (Chernyshevsky, with the same qualities and also courting danger as leader of the radicals, ends up in Petropavlovsk Fortress / Siberia); undeterred by his predicament, Ivan Matveich seeks to take advantage of his "martyrdom" and preach his progressive ideas to the world from within the belly of the crocodile (Chernyshevsky, unrestrained by imprisonment, preaches his progressive ideas to the world in *What Is To Be Done?* which is written from within the "belly" of state imprisonment); Ivan Matveich's wife refuses to join him in the belly of the crocodile and takes advantage of her new-found status as the "semi-widow" of a famous man (Chernyshevsky's wife presumably does not follow him into exile and "enjoys" her new status); etc., etc.

Allegory, unfortunately, can be the overactive offspring of a heated mind seeking hidden meaning where none exists. Once the allegory is suggested, however, it can assume an independent and unrelated life of its own. Despite claiming a cordial relationship with and respect for Chernyshevsky, Dostoevsky, that master purveyor of twisted and torturous psychological relationships, might well have harbored more ambiguous feelings about the man. At the risk of further distorting what might already be a complete distortion of Dostoevsky's intent in writing "The Crocodile", here are a few cryptic lines from Dostoevsky's unpublished notebooks during the conception period of "The Crocodile" that are suggestive when one considers that Dostoevsky saw Chernyshevsky as a leader of the nihilists: "Socialism posits the goal of a *full belly* as the whole future basis and standard of the social anthill . . . First the nihilists. I came to ask you about the structure (?) of the crocodile."[1] As to the question of Dostoevsky's magnanimity, here is another suggestive passage from the same source: "I regret the untimely death of

1. Proffer, Carl (ed.). *The Unpublished Dostoevsky. Diaries and Notebooks (*1860-81*).* 3 Volumes. Ann Arbor, 1973. I, 98.

Dobrolyubov[2] and others, both personally and as writers. But I won't say that they didn't lie just because of this regret."[3]

2. Dobrolyubov, Nikolai Aleksandrovich (1836-61). Radical critic and follower of Chernyshevsky. Endorsed the older radical's materialist philosophy in dealing with art and literature. Dobrolyubov's most famous work, "What is Oblomovism?", concerned a study of the Russian literary "superfluous man" and I. A. Goncharov's novel, *Oblomov*.

3. *The Unpublished Dostoevsky*, I, 104.

THE CROCODILE

AN UNUSUAL INCIDENT OR AN ARCANE AFFAIR AT THE ARCADE[1]

*a truthful story about how one gentleman,
of a certain age and a certain appearance,
was swallowed alive by a crocodile,
without a single trace, and what came out*

*Ohé, Lambert! Où est Lambert?
As-tu vu Lambert?*[2]

CHAPTER I

On the thirteenth of January, in the current year of [eighteen] sixty-five, at half-past twelve, p.m., Yelena Ivanovna, the spouse of Ivan Matveich who was my educated friend, colleague and rather distant relation, wished to view the crocodile which was being displayed for a certain price in *The Arcade*. With a ticket to go abroad already in hand (not so much for reasons of illness as of inquisitiveness), and consequently, already considering himself on leave in regard to work, and, therefore, being completely free on that morning, not only did Ivan Matveich not impede the vague desire of his spouse in the least, but was seized with curiosity himself. "A marvellous idea," he said expansively. "Let us examine the crocodile! In view of the fact that we are setting off for Europe, it would not be amiss to become acquainted on the spot with the natives who inhabit it,"—and with those words, taking his spouse under his

3

arm, he thereupon set out for *The Arcade* with her. For my part, as was my custom, I insisted on joining them—in the role of a family friend. Never before had I seen Ivan Matveich in a more pleasant frame of mind as on that morning so memorable for me,—how true that we have no foreknowledge of our fate! Upon entering *The Arcade*, he immediately became enraptured with the magnificence of the building, and approaching the shop wherein the monster, newly imported to the capital, was being displayed, he himself wished to pay the crocodile keeper my quarter-rouble admission: something which had never happened in the past. Entering a large room, we remarked that in addition to the crocodile it also contained parrots of a foreign species, a cockatoo and, moreover, a group of monkeys in a separate cage at the back. Right at the very entrance, by the left-hand wall, stood a large tin box somewhat in the form of a bath tub, covered with a strong metal screen, and with several inches of water in the bottom. In this rather shallow pond was kept the most enormous crocodile which was lying there like a log, completely motionlesss, and, apparently, deprived of all its faculties due to that climate of ours which is so damp and inhospitable to foreigners. At first this monster did not arouse any particular curiosity in any of us.

"So this is supposed to be the crocodile!" Yelena Ivanovna said with pity in a sing-song voice. "But I thought that it was . . . somehow different!"

In all likelihood she thought that it was stunning. The German, who was both the host and owner of the crocodile, had appeared before us and was staring at us with a look of extreme pride.

"He is right," Ivan Matveich whispered to me, "because he is aware that he is the only one in all of Russia who has a crocodile on display now."

I attributed this utterly absurd remark as well to the extremely benevolent mood which had overcome Ivan Matveich, who in other circumstances was highly envious.

"It seems to me that your crocodile is not alive," Yelena Ivanovna declared once more, piqued by the owner's unresponsiveness, as she addressed him with a gracious smile—a manouever so characteristic of women.

"Oh, no, Madame," he responded in broken Russian and thereupon started to poke the crocodile in the head after raising the screen on the box halfway.

Then the wily monster, in order to show signs of life, barely moved its feet and tail, raised its snout and emitted something in the nature of an extended wheezing sound.

"Now, do not be angry, Karlchen!" said the German tenderly with self-satisfied vanity.

"What a repulsive crocodile it is! I was even frightened," Yelena Ivanovna prattled even more coquettishly. "Now I am going to have dreams about it."

"But he vill not bite you in your dreams, Madame," rejoined the German gallantly and was the first to laugh at the wit of his own words, but none of us responded.

"Let's go, Semyon Semyonich," Yelena Ivanovna

continued, turning her exclusive attention to me. "Better we take a look at the monkeys. I just adore monkeys, some of them are such darlings . . . but the crocodile is horrible."

"Oh, fear not, my friend," Ivan Matveich shouted after us as he delighted in a show of bravery before his spouse. "This slumberous denizen of the kingdom of the pharaohs won't do anything to us," and he remained behind by the box. Moreover, he took his glove and started to tickle the crocodile's nose with it, wishing, as he admitted afterward, to make it emit another wheezing sound. As for the owner, he had followed Yelena Ivanovna, since she was the lady, to the cage with the monkeys.

All was proceeding marvellously in this fashion and it was impossible to foresee anything. Yelena Ivanovna was playfully amusing herself with the monkeys and it seemed as though she were totally absorbed in them. She was squealing with pleasure, continually addressing me as though she had no wish to take any notice of the owner, and laughing at the resemblance which she discerned between these marmosets and her close friends and acquaintances. I, too, was completely caught up in the merriment, for the resemblance was beyond any doubt. The German-proprietor did not know whether he should laugh or not and for that reason there was a frown on his face towards the end. And lo, at that very moment, the room was suddenly shaken by a horrible, I might even add, unnatural cry. Without knowing what to think, I at first froze on the spot; but remarking that it was in fact Yelena Ivanovna who was screaming, I quickly turned around and—what did I see! I saw—oh, Lord—I saw, in the horrible jaws of the crocodile, the unfortunate Ivan Matveich, whose torso had been seized crosswise and who was now raised horizontally in the air and desperately dangling his legs. An instant later—and he was gone. But I shall describe in detail because all the while I was standing there motionless and I managed to follow the entire process transpiring before me with an attentiveness and curiosity that eludes me even now. ("For," I was thinking in that fateful moment, "what if all of this were happening to me instead of Ivan Matveich—what an unpleasant business that would be for me!"). But down to business. The crocodile had begun by turning the unfortunate Ivan Matveich in its terrible jaws feet first towards itself, next it swallowed the legs themselves; then, belching Ivan Matveich out a bit who was trying to jump out and was hanging on to the box with his hands, it once again drew him inside to a point above his waist. Then, after another belch, it swallowed again and again. In this fashion Ivan Matveich visibly disappeared before our eyes. At last, with one final swallow, the crocodile consumed my entire educated friend, and, this time without a trace. From the crocodile's exterior one could remark on how all the varying shapes of Ivan Matveich were passing through its innards. I was about to start shouting anew when suddenly fate once again exhibited its perfidious desire to mock us: the crocodile contracted, probably choking from the enormity of the object that it had swallowed, opened wide its terrifying jaws once more, and in the form of a final belch, Ivan

Matveich's head suddenly popped out for a single instant bearing a look of despair, whereupon his spectacles instantly tumbled from his nose to the bottom of the box. It seemed that this desperate head had popped up for the sole purpose of casting one final glance at all things and mentally to bid farewell to all worldly pleasures. But it did not succeed in its intention: once more the crocodile summoned its strength, swallowed—and in a flash the head had disappeared once more, this time once and for all. This appearance and disappearance of a still living human head was so horrible, and yet at the same time—whether because of the speed or unexpectedness of the action, or in consequence of the spectacles falling from the nose—it contained in itself something that was so amusing that I suddenly and quite unexpectedly giggled. But recollecting immediately that it was unseemly of me to laugh at that particular moment by virtue of being a family friend, I immediately turned to Yelena Ivanovna and with an expression of sympathy I said to her:

"Now our Ivan Matveich is *kaput*!"

I cannot even imagine trying to express just how powerful was Yelena Ivanovna's agitation during the course of the entire process. At first, after the initial scream, it was as though she had become frozen on the spot and was watching the commotion being presented to her with apparent indifference, yet with eyes bulging wide in the extreme; then she suddenly dissolved in a rending shriek, but I seized her by the hands. In that instant the owner himself, who at first had also been stunned in horror, suddenly clapped his hands and started to shout as he gazed heavenward:

"Ach, my crocodile, ach, mein allerliebster Karlchen! Mutter, mutter, mutter!"

The rear door was opened in response to this cry and the mother appeared in a bonnet, ruddy-cheeked, elderly, but disheveled, and with a screech she dashed to her German.

At this point all Sodom broke loose: Yelena Ivanovna kept screaming a single phrase: "Whip it! Whip it!" And she kept rushing up to the owner and the mother, apparently beseeching them—probably in all self-obliviousness—to whip someone for something. But the owner and the mother paid neither of us any attention: they were both wailing like calves around the box.

"For goot he is gone, now he split open because he has svallowed a whole official!" The owner kept shouting.

"Unser Karlchen, unser allerliebster Karlchen wird sterben!" The mistress wailed.

"Now vee are orfans and have no brot!" The owner joined in.

"Whip it, whip it, whip it!" Yelena Ivanovna babbled as she fastened on to the German's frock coat.

"He vas teasing de crocodile. Why your husband he tease de crocodile!" The German kept shouting as he tried to free himself. "You vill pay if Karlchen vill go kaput. Das war mein Sohn, das war mein einziger Sohn!"

I must admit that I was terribly indignant seeing this kind of egoism from that German foreigner and the hardheartedness of his disheveled mother. Nonetheless, Yelena Ivanovna's endlessly repeated cries of "whip it, whip it!" aroused my anxiety even more and finally distracted me so entirely that I began to fear that . . . I shall say right away that I utterly miscomprehended these strange outcries: it had seemed to me that Yelena Ivanovna had lost her reason for an instant, but, nevertheless wishing to have revenge for the demise of her beloved Ivan Matveich, she was suggesting that by way of the satisfaction that was her due the crocodile should be punished with a whipping. Yet all the while she had meant something completely different. As I cast a glance at the door with some embarrassment, I began to entreat Yelena Ivanovna to calm herself and, most importantly, not to use that delicate word "whip". For, that kind of retrograde wish here in the very heart of *The Arcade* and in the midst of educated society, a step away from that same hall where perhaps at this very moment Mr. Lavrov[3] was reading a public lecture, was not only impossible but even unthinkable, and, at any moment could make us objects for the caricatures of Mister Stepanov[4] and attract jeers for being unenlightened. To my horror, those fearful suspicions of mine were immediately proven correct: suddenly the curtain, which separated the crocodile room from the entrance hall where the quarter-roubles were collected, was parted and there appeared a figure with a beard and moustache, holding a peaked cap and making a concerted effort to bend well forward with the upper part of his body while at the same time taking every precaution to keep his feet on the other side of the entrance into the crocodile room so that he would maintain the right not to have to pay the admission fee.

"Madame, that kind of retrograde desire," said the stranger who was trying somehow not to tumble over in our direction and keep his distance on the other side of the threshold, "does no honor to your development and is conditioned by the lack of phosphorus in your brain tissue. You will be jeered immediately in the chronicles of progress and in the satirical tabloids of our . . ."

But he did not finish: the owner, who had come to his senses and who in horror had caught sight of a person talking in the crocodile room without having paid anything, hurled himself in a frenzy at the progressive stranger and chucked him out with both hands. For a moment both disappeared from our eyes beyond the curtain and it was only then that I finally surmised that the whole commotion had arisen out of nothing. Yelena Ivanovna was completely innocent: by no means had she intended, as I had already remarked above, to subjugate the crocodile to a retrograde and humiliating punishment, that is, to *whip* it. Rather, quite simply, she had wished merely to have someone *rip*[5] open the belly with a knife and thus release Ivan Matveich from the innards.

"Vat! You vant that my crocodile should be dead!" The owner who had come running back started to wail. "No, first let your husband be dead, and then the crocodile! . . . Mein Vater he showed the crocodile, mein

Grossvater he showed the crocodile, mein Sohn he vill be showing the crocodile, and I be showing the crocodile! Everybody vill be showing the crocodile! I for all Europe am famous, but you for all Europe are not famous and damages you must pay me."

"Ja, ja!" The malicious old German woman joined in. "You vee not let go, damage if Karlchen split open!"

"It's useless to disembowel it," I added calmly, wishing to divert Yelena Ivanovna homeward as quickly as possible. "In all probability our dear Ivan Matveich is now soaring somewhere in the empyrean."

"My friend," at that moment, quite unexpectedly, we heard Ivan Matveich's voice which utterly dumbfounded us, "my friend, I am of the opinion that we must act directly through the bureau of the chief inspector, for this German will not comprehend the truth without the aid of the police."

These words, spoken firmly, authoritatively and expressing an unusual presence of mind, so dumbfounded us at first that we were all on the point of refusing to believe our ears. But, naturally, we immediately ran up to the box with the crocodile, and, as much in awe as disbelief, we listened to the unfortunate prisoner. His voice was muffled, thin, even shrill, as though originating at some significant distance from us. It was reminiscent of the situation when some jokester, going off into another room and covering his mouth with an ordinary bed pillow, would start to shout, wishing to represent to the company remaining behind in the other room how two peasants would hail each other when out in the wilderness or separated by a deep ravine. This was something I had had the pleasure of hearing once at my acquaintance's during yuletide.

"Ivan Matveich, my friend, so you are alive then!" Yelena Ivanovna murmured.

"Alive and well," Ivan Matveich replied. "And thanks to the Most High I have been swallowed without any damage. The one thing that does disturb me is how the authorities will view this episode. Having received my ticket to go abroad I ended up in a crocodile, which was not very clever at all . . ."

"But, my friend, don't concern yourself with being witty. The main thing is to pluck you out of there somehow," Yelena Ivanovna interrupted.

"Pluck!" the owner screeched. "I von't allow you to pluck crocodile. Now much more public vill come and I vill ask for fuenfzig kopecks and Karlchen vill not split open."

"Gott sei dank!" The mistress added.

"They are right," Ivan Matveich calmly remarked. "The principle of economics comes first."

"My friend," I cried, "I will fly this very moment to the authorities and complain, for I have a premonition that that we won't be able to straighten out this mess ourselves."

"And I think likewise," Ivan Matveich remarked. "But without any economic compensation it will be difficult in our age of commercial crisis to disembowel a crocodile *gratis*, and, in the meantime, the unavoidable question is posed: what will the owner take for his crocodile? And the next question: who will pay? For you know that I do not have any means . . ."

"How can payment even be a consideration," I remarked timidly. But the owner interrupted me immediately:

"I vill not sell the crocodile, I vill sell the crocodile for three thousand, I vill sell the crocodile for four thousand! Now the public vill come very much. I vill sell the crocodile for five thousand!"

In short, he was playing the unbearable bully. Self-interest and vile avarice shone joyfully in his eyes.

"I am away!" I shouted indignantly.

"And I! I too! I shall go to Andrei Osipich, I shall soften him with my tears," whimpered Yelena Ivanovna.

"Don't do that, my friend," Ivan Matveich hastily interrupted her. For a long while now he had been jealous of his spouse together with Andrei Osipich and knew that she would be happy to make the trip in order to shed some tears before an educated man because tears were very becoming to her. Turning to me he continued: "And I advise you to the contrary. There is no point in going off without rhyme or reason. Something will still come of this. Better you drop in on Timofei Semyonich today by way of a private visit. He is an old-fashioned person and none-too-clever, but he is solid, and, most importantly, he is sincere. Give him my respects and describe the circumstances of the case. Since I owe him seven roubles for our last card game, pass it on to him in this convenient situation: that will soften the stern old man. In any event, we can gain direction from his advice. And now take Yelena Ivanovna away for the time being . . . Calm yourself, my friend," he continued to her. "I am tired from all the shouting and squabbling of old wives and I wish to doze a bit. It's warm and soft here although I have not yet managed to examine my surroundings in this sanctuary wherein I find myself so unexpectedly . . ."

"Examine your surroundings! Do you really find it so light there?" Yelena Ivanovna cried out with delight.

"I am surrounded by impenetrable night," replied the poor prisoner. "But I can touch and so to speak examine my surroundings with my hands . . . Farewell, be calm and don't deprive yourself of amusements. Until tomorrow! And you, Semyon Semyonich, come visit me in the evening. Since you are distracted and might forget, tie a string around your finger . . ."

I must admit that I was happy to leave because I was too exhausted, and, to a degree, weary of all this as well. Hastily I took under my arm a Yelena Ivanovna who was despondent and yet who had grown attractive from the agitation and I quickly escorted her out of the crocodile room.

"In the evening another quarter-rouble for the entrance!" The owner shouted after us.

"Oh, Lord, how greedy they are!" Yelena Ivanovna declared as she glanced at herself in every mirror on the walls of *The Arcade*, apparently aware of the fact that her looks had improved.

"The principle of economics," I replied with a gentle excitement, taking pride in my lady before the passers-by.

"The principle of economics," she drawled in her sympathetic little voice. "I understood nothing of what

Ivan Matveich was saying just now concerning this repulsive principle of economics."

"I shall explain to you," I replied and immediately began to talk about the beneficial results of attracting foreign capital to our fatherland, which I had just read about that morning in *The Petersburg News* and *The Hair*.[6]

"How strange it all is!" She interrupted me after listening for a while. "But do stop, you repulsive man. What nonsense you're speaking . . . Tell me, how do I seem to you?"

"You are quite seemly!" I remarked, exploiting the situation in order to deliver a compliment.

"Naughty man!" She murmured with satisfaction. "Poor Ivan Matveich," she added after a moment, her head coquettishly inclined towards her shoulder. "Truly, I do feel sorry for him. Oh, my Lord!" She suddenly cried. "Tell me, how is he going to eat there today and . . . and . . . how will he . . . what if he needs anything?"

"An unforeseen question," I replied, also puzzled. In truth, that had not entered my mind. Women are that much more practical than we men for solving everyday problems!

"The poor fellow, the way he's ended up . . . nothing to amuse himself with and the darkness . . . how vexing that I don't have a photograph left of him . . . So, now I'm rather like a widow," she added with a seductive smile, obviously interested in her new situation. "Hm . . . all the same I do feel sorry for him . . ."

In short, this was an expression of a young and interesting wife's understandable and natural grief for her deceased husband. I finally brought her home, consoled her and after dining together with her and drinking a cup of aromatic coffee, I set out at six o'clock for Timofei Semyonich's, reckoning that at that hour all family people of specific occupations would be sitting or lying around their homes.

Having written this first chapter in a style befitting the related event, I now intend to employ a style which, although not as elevated, is, nevertheless, more natural and about which I am informing the reader in advance.

CHAPTER II

The esteemed Timofei Semyonich greeted me rather hastily, and, consequently, with some confusion. He led me into his cramped study and firmly closed the door: ("So the children won't interfere," he declared with visible agitation). Thereupon he seated me on a chair by the desk and he himself sat in an armchair, closed the flaps of his old padded housecoat and assumed a kind of official, almost stern expression just in case, although he was neither Ivan Matveich's superior nor mine, but up until then had considered himself an ordinary colleague and even an acquaintance.

"First of all," he began, "bear in mind that I am not one of the authorities, but the same kind of subordinate as both you and Ivan Matveich . . . I do not intend to get involved in anything."

I was amazed that apparently he already knew everything. Despite this fact I gave a fresh and detailed account of the story. I even spoke with emotion, for at that moment I was fulfilling the responsiblity of a true friend. He heard me out without any particular amazement, rather with a manifest sign of suspiciousness.

"Just imagine," he said after listening to me, "I always supposed that invariably this would happen to him."

"Whatever for, Timofei Semyonich? The incident in itself is unusual in the extreme . . ."

"I agree. But during the entire course of his service Ivan Matveich was bound to come precisely to such an end. Dexterous, presumptuous even. Always 'progress' and various ideas, but that's what progress leads to!"

"But after all this is a most unusual incident and it's quite impossible to consider this as a general rule for all progressives . . ."

"But that's how it is. You see, it comes from being overeducated, believe me. Because people who are overeducated intrude everywhere and most of all where they have no business. However, perhaps you know more," he added as though offended. "I am a person who doesn't have that much education and I am old. I served in the ranks as an army school child[7] and have reached my fiftieth anniversary in the service this year."

"But no, Timofei Semyonich, for goodness' sake . . . on the contrary, Ivan Matveich longs for your advice, he longs for your guidance. Even to the point of tears, so to speak."

"'Even to the point of tears, so to speak.' Hm. Well, those are just crocodile tears and one can't believe them entirely. Just tell me what, then, attracted him abroad? And where did he get the money? He doesn't have the means, does he?"

"From his savings, Timofei Semyonich, from the recent bonuses," I replied plaintively. "He only wanted to go for three months, all told, to Switzerland . . . to William Tell's homeland."

"William Tell? Hm!"

"He wanted to greet the springtime in Napoli. To examine the museums, the customs, the animals . . ."

"Hm! The animals? And don't we have enough animals here? There are menageries, museums, camels. Bears live right outside of Petersburg itself. And just look, he himself took up residence in a crocodile.."

"Timofei Semyonich, for goodness' sake, a person finds himself in misfortune, a person comes running as though to a friend, as though to an older relative, he longs for advice, and you, you are reproaching him . . . At least have pity on the wretched Yelena Ivanovna!"

"You mean the spouse? An interesting lady," Timofei declared, apparently softening and taking his snuff with relish. "A slip of a thing. Full-breasted and always tilting her head to the side like this, yes, to the side . . . very nice. Andrei Osipich was mentioning her just the other day."

"Mentioning her?"

"Yes, he was, and in terms that were highly flattering. The bust, he said, the glance, the hair style . . . A confection, he said, and not a little lady, and at that point they started to laugh. They're still young people." Timofei Semyonich blew his nose with gusto. "Incidentally, that's a fine young man, and what careers they're making for themselves . . ."

"But after all we're talking about something different here, Timofei Semyonich."

"Of course, of course."

"So what now, Timofei Semyonich?"

"But what can I possibly do?"

"Give us advice, guide us, like a man of experience, like a relative! What should we undertake? Should we go to the authorities or . . ."

"To the authorities? Absolutely not," Timofei Semyonich stated. "If you wish my advice, then above all this business must be hushed up and you must act as a private individual. This incident is suspicious and without precedent. The main thing, it's without precedent, there's been nothing like it and that is not in its favor . . . Therefore, caution above all else . . . Just let him lie there by himself for a while. He must bide his time, just bide his time . . ."

"But how is he to bide his time, Timofei Semyonich? What if he suffocates there?"

"But why should he? It seems you yourself said that he had settled in even with a certain amount of comfort."

I related everything once more. Timofei Semyonich grew pensive.

"Hm!," he declared, turning the snuff box around in his hands. "In my opinion it's not at all bad that he'll be lying there for a while instead of being abroad. Let him give it some thought at his leisure. Naturally, he must not suffocate, and for that reason the appropriate measures must be taken to protect his health. You know, to beware of a cough and so forth . . . As far as the German is concerned, it is my personal opinion that he is in his rights, and more so than the other party, because someone crawled into *his* crocodile without permission, whereas *he* was not the one who crawled into Ivan Matveich's crocodile, who, by the way, insofar as I recall, had no crocodile. Well, and the crocodile constitutes property, as it were, and it cannot be cut up without compensation."

"To rescue humanity, Timofei Semyonich?"

"Now that's an affair for the police. That's to whom it should be addressed."

"But Ivan Matveich might be needed at our office. They might ask for him."

"Ivan Matveich needed? Hee-hee! But after all he's supposed to be on leave, consequently, we can disregard that. Let him have a look at the European countries over there. It's a different matter if he doesn't show up after his time is up. Then we can ask questions and make inquiries . . ."

"But that's three months! Timofei Semyonich, for goodness' sake!"

"He himself is to blame. Well, who stuck him in there? So, very likely he'll have to hire a public nurse, and there's no provision for that on our staff. The main thing is that the crocodile is property; consequently, we are confronting the so-called principle of economics in action. And the principle of economics comes first. Just the day before yesterday Ignaty Prokofyich was talking at an evening at Luka Andreich's. You know Ignaty Prokofyich? A capitalist, up on things, and, you know, he spoke well when he said that we need industry. We don't have enough industry, he said. We have to give rise to it. We have to give rise to capital. That means we have to give rise to a middle class, the so-called bourgeoisie. And since we don't have capital, that means we have to attract it from abroad. First of all we must make way for foreign companies to buy up parcels of our land as has been confirmed everywhere abroad now. Communal property is poison, he said, it means ruin! And you know he was saying this with such feeling. Well, that's fine for them, I suppose, they're people of capital . . . they're not government servants. With communal property-holding, he said, neither industry nor agriculture will be advanced. Foreign companies must be allowed, wherever possible, to buy up our entire country bit by bit, he said, and then to divide it up and go on dividing it up as much as possible into tiny portions. And you know he pronounced it emphatically like that: *di–i–vide*. Then we must sell it off as private property. And not just sell it off, but only rent it out. When the entire land is in the hands of the foreign companies who have been attracted here, then it would mean that it would be possible to set whatever price you wished for the rent. Consequently, the peasant will work three times as much just for his daily bread and he can be dismissed at will. That means he will be sensible, submissive, diligent and will produce three times as much for the same cost. And what good is he in the commune now! He knows that he won't starve to death, so he's just lazy and drinks all the while.

Meanwhile we'll be attracting money, capital will be expanded and the bourgeoisie will emerge. Over there the English political and literary newspaper *The Times* was discussing our finances and concluded the other day that our finances were not growing because we had no middle class, there were no large purses of money and we didn't have an obliging proletariat . . . Ignaty Prokofyich put it well. He's an orator. He himself wants to state his opinion to the authorities and then publish it in *The* [Petersburg] *News*. It wouldn't be just a bunch of verses in the style of Ivan Matveich . . ."

"But what about Ivan Matveich?" I interjected, having let the old man babble on. Timofei Semyonich sometimes loved to babble on and thereby show that he was not backward and knew all about these things.

"Ivan Matveich? I'm getting to that. Here we are making an effort to attract foreign capital to the fatherland and now judge for yourself: the capital of this crocodile which we've attracted here has only just doubled, due to Ivan Matveich, and rather than protecting foreign property, here we are trying to disembowel that very same basic capital. Now does that make sense? In my opinion, Ivan Matveich, as a true son of the fatherland, should rejoice even more so and be proud of the fact that by means of himself he has doubled the value of the foreign crocodile and even most likely tripled it. That is what is needed to attract capital. If one is successful, before you know it, a second arrives with a crocodile, then a third brings two or three at once and capital starts to accumulate around them. And there you have your bourgeoisie. Incentives are required."

"For goodness' sake, Timofei Semyonich!" I cried. "What you're demanding is an almost unnatural self-sacrifice on the part of the wretched Ivan Matveich!"

"I am demanding nothing of the sort and, above all, I beg you, as I did earlier, to consider that I am not one of the authorities and, consequently, I cannot demand anything from anyone. I am speaking as a son of the fatherland, that is, I am not speaking as the *Son of the Fatherland*,[8] but simply as *a* son of the fatherland. Besides, who ordered him to crawl into the crocodile? A reliable person, a person of a certain rank, in a state of legal matrimony, and suddenly, he takes a step like that! Does that make sense?"

"But, after all, that step happened quite unexpectedly."

"Who can say? Moreover, where is the money coming from to pay the crocodile owner, just tell me that?"

"Is it really a question of payment, Timofei Semyonich?"

"Can he get it?"

"No, he can't." I replied sadly. "At first the crocodile owner was afraid that the crocodile would split open, but then when he was convinced that all was well, he put on airs and rejoiced that he could double the price."

"Triple it, or even quadruple it! The public will come in a flood now. Those crocodile owners are a clever people. Moreover, they're carnivores and have a tendency towards amusement, and for that reason I repeat: above all let Ivan Matveich maintain his incognito, do not let him be in a hurry. Even if everyone most likely knows that he's inside the crocodile, still they don't know officially. In this regard, Ivan Matveich even finds himself in favorable circumstances, because he is deemed to be abroad. People will say that he is inside the crocodile, but we can refuse to believe it. That is how we can respond. The main thing is to have him bide his time. Besides, where can he be in such a rush to get to?"

"But what if . . ."

"Don't worry, he has a solid constitution . . ."

"Well what about after he has bided his time?"

"I won't conceal from you that this incident is complicated in the extreme. It's impossible to fully imagine, and the main thing is—what is harmful—is the fact that up until now there hasn't been a case like it. If there had been such a case, then we might find some kind of direction. Otherwise, how is one to decide what to do here? As soon as you start to weigh the matter, it gets complicated."

A happy thought flashed through my mind.

"Couldn't it be so arranged," I said, "that if he's fated to remain in the bowels of the monster, and, by the will of Providence, his life is preserved, would it not be possible to give him permission to be counted at work?"

"Hm . . . you mean in the form of leave without pay?"

"No. Couldn't it be arranged with pay?"

"On what basis?"

"In the form of an official business trip . . ."

"What kind and where to?"

"Into the crocodile, into the bowels of the crocodile . . . To gather information, so to speak, to study the facts on the spot. Of course, it would be novel, but it is progressive and at the same time it would show a solicitude for enlightenment . . ."

Timofei Semyonich grew pensive.

"To dispatch a special official," he said at last, "into the bowels of a crocodile on a special assignment—in my personal opinion, that is absurd. There is no provision for that on staff. What kind of assignment could take him there?"

"For a natural, so to speak, study of nature on the spot, inside living matter. Nowadays the natural sciences, botany, are in vogue . . . He would be living there and passing on information . . . say, about digestion or habits. In order to accumulate facts."

"In other words, it would be in the realm of statistics. Well, that's not my strong point and I'm no philosopher. 'Facts' you say. As it is we're inundated with facts and don't know what to do with them. Moreover, these statistics are dangerous . . ."

"In what way?"

"Just because. And furthermore, you must admit that he'll be passing on the facts while lying down, so to speak. And can a person really be working while he's lying down? Now that would be yet another innovation, and, moreover, a very dangerous one. Besides, there's no precedent for it. Now if only we had even the slightest kind of precedent, then, in my opinion, it might be possible to organize an official trip for him."

"But, Timofei Semyonich, no living crocodiles have ever been brought here until now."

"Hm, yes . . ." He grew pensive once more. "If you

like, this objection of yours is justified and could even serve as the basis for pursuing the case further. But again you must consider that if with the appearance of live crocodiles government officials begin to disappear, and then, on the basis of the fact that it's warm and soft there they demand to be put on special assignment and while lying down . . . you yourself must agree that it's a bad example. Then likely everyone would try to get in there to be paid for nothing."

"Do what you can, Timofei Semyonich! Incidentally, Ivan Matveich asked me to pay you what he owes you for cards, the seven roubles he lost at whist . . ."

"Ah, he lost that the other day at Nikifor Nikiforich's! I remember. How cheerful he was then, so amusing, and now!.."

The old man was genuinely moved.

"Do what you can, Timofei Semyonich."

"I'll lend my assistance. I'll have a talk on my own initiative, in a private fashion, as though making inquiries. Incidentally, find out unofficially, on the side, exactly what price the owner would accept for his crocodile."

Timofei Semyonich had apparently softened.

"Immediately," I replied. "And I'll come back to you at once with the answer."

"The spouse . . . is she by herself now? Is she bored?"

"You ought to pay her a visit, Timofei Semyonich."

"I will. Just recently I was thinking of doing so and this would be a convenient occasion . . . And whatever made him go and see the crocodile! Incidentally, I would like to take a look at it myself."

"Do go and visit the poor fellow, Timofei Semyonich."

"I will. Of course I don't want to raise any hopes by doing so. I'll go as a private individual . . . Well, good-bye, I'm off to Nikifor Nikiforich's again. Will you come along?"

"No, I'm off to the prisoner."

"Yes, off to the prisoner now! My, my, what frivolousness!"

I bid farewell to the old man. Various thoughts were going through my head. Timofei Semyonich was a kind and most honest person, yet, as I left him, I was nevertheless happy that he had already passed his fiftieth anniversary and that the Timofei Semyoniches were now a rarity among us. Naturally I immediately flew off to *The Arcade* to communicate everything to the poor wretch, Ivan Matveich. Moreover, I was seized with curiosity: how had he settled down in the crocodile and how was it possible to live inside a crocodile? Was it really possible to live inside a crocodile? Truly, at times it seemed to me that this was all some kind of monstrous dream, all the more so because it did concern a monster . . .

CHAPTER III

However, it was not a dream, but genuine, unquestionable reality. Otherwise, would I even be telling it! But let me continue . . .

I arrived at *The Arcade* late, around nine o'clock and I was obliged to enter the crocodile room from the rear entrance because the German had locked up the shop earlier this time than was the custom. He was strutting about in domestic garb, wearing some kind of an old soiled frock coat, yet he was three times more satisfied than earlier in the morning. It was apparent that he no longer feared anything and that "much public had come". The mother appeared later, obviously in order to keep an eye on me. The German frequently exchanged whispers with his mother. Despite the fact that the shop was already closed, he nevertheless took a quarter-rouble from me. What unnecessary scrupulousness!

"Each time you vill pay; the public, it vill pay a

rouble, but only you vill pay one quarter-rouble, because you are good friend of your good friend, and I respect friend . . ."

"Is he alive, is my educated friend alive!" I cried loudly, going up to the crocodile and hoping that my words would reach Ivan Matveich from afar and flatter his vanity.

"Alive and well," he replied, as though from afar, or seemingly from beneath a bed, although I was standing alongside him. "Alive and well, but about that later . . . How do things stand?"

Purposely pretending not to have heard the question, I was about to begin a hasty and solicitous questioning of my own: namely, how he was, what he was doing, how it was inside the crocodile and generally what was inside the crocodile? I posed all of this with my customary civility and affability. But he interrupted me in a manner both irritated and capricious.

"How do things stand?" He cried, ordering me about, as was his custom, in that shrill voice of his which now seemed repulsive in the extreme.

I related my entire conversation with Timofei Semyonich down to the last detail. As I did so, I tried to impart a slightly insulted tone.

"The old man is right," Ivan Matveich concluded with the same abruptness that always typified his conversation with me. "I like practical people and I cannot bear sentimental milksops. I am prepared as well, however, to recognize that your idea concerning the official assignment is not utterly absurd. Actually there is a great deal that I can communicate both in a scientific as well as in a moral regard. But now all of this is assuming a new and unexpected form and it is not worth it to make any petition simply for reasons of recompense. Listen carefully. Are you sitting down?"

"No, I'm standing."

"Sit down on something, on the floor if necessary, and listen carefully."

Angrily I took a chair and in a fit of temper I banged it on the floor as I set it down.

"Listen," he began in a peremptory tone. "The public came in masses today. By evening there wasn't enough space and the police appeared for the sake of order. At eight o'clock, that is, earlier than usual, the owner even found it necessary to close the shop and terminate the presentation in order to count the money which had accumulated and to prepare more conveniently for tomorrow. I know that it will be like a carnival here tomorrow. Thus, one must suppose that all the most educated people of the capital, ladies of higher society, foreign ambassadors, the legal profession and so forth will pay a visit. Moreover, people will start coming from the most diverse provinces of our vast and curious empire. As a result, I shall be on display to all, and although concealed, nevertheless I shall be of paramount importance. I shall instruct the idle crowd. Schooled by experience, I shall make of myself an example of grandeur and submission before fate! I shall be, so to speak, a pulpit wherefrom I shall begin to instruct humanity. Even the information from the natural sciences which I can pass on is precious. Therefore, not only do I not grumble at the recent incident, but I firmly hope to make the most brilliant of careers."

"You wouldn't be finding it dull in there?" I remarked venomously.

I was chafed most of all by the fact that he kept referring to himself over and over again in such self-important terms. Nevertheless, I was bewildered by all of this. ("What's making this frivolous dolt put on such airs?" I whispered to myself as I gnashed my teeth. "He should be weeping rather than putting on airs.")

"No!" He replied sharply to my remark. "Because I am brimming over with mighty ideas. Only now am I able to dream at leisure about improving the fate of all of mankind. Truth and light will now issue forth from a crocodile. There is no doubt that I shall devise my own theory of economic relationships and I shall be proud of it—which is something that hitherto I have been unable to do because of the vulgar amusements of society and the lack of leisure enforced by having to work. I shall revolutionize everything and I shall become the new Fourier.[9] Incidentally, did you give the seven roubles to Timofei Semyonich?"

"Out of my own pocket," I replied, trying to emphasize with my voice that I had indeed paid out of my own pocket.

"Accounts will be rendered," he replied condescendingly. "I expect a salary bonus without fail, for who should receive a bonus if not I? Now my utility is unlimited. But down to business. The wife?"

"You are probably asking about Yelena Ivanovna?"

"The wife?!" He started to shout in what was almost a shriek this time.

I had no choice! Submissively, but again gnashing my teeth, I related to him how I had left Yelena Ivanovna. He did not even let me finish.

"I have particular designs for her," he began impatiently. "If I shall be famous *here*, then I want her to be famous *there*. Scholars, poets, philosophers, foreign mineralogists, and gentlemen of state will visit her salon in the evenings after their morning conversations with me. Commencing next week she must begin to hold a salon every evening. My doubled salary will provide the means for holding receptions, and insofar as the receptions are to be restricted to tea alone and served by hired lackeys, then that should take care of that. I will be the topic of conversation both here and there. For a long while I have been craving the opportunity to have everyone talk about me, but I was unable to achieve this by virtue of my unimportance and insufficient rank. But now all of this has been achieved apparently by what is the simplest swallow of a crocodile. My every word will be listened to attentively, every utterance will be pondered, passed on and printed. And I shall make myself known! People will comprehend at last what capabilities they have allowed to disappear into the bowels of a monster. 'This man might have been a foreign minister and governed a kingdom,' they will say. 'This man did not succeed in governing a foreign kingdom,' others will say. But then am I worse than any of those people like Garnier-Pagès[10] . . . or whatever their names are over there . . . My wife must con-

stitute a *pendant* for me: I have the intellect whereas she
has beauty and graciousness. 'She is beautiful, hence she
is his wife,' some will say. 'She is beautiful *because she is
his wife*,' others will correct them. In any event have
Yelena Ivanovna buy, no later than tomorrow, the
encyclopaedic dictionary[11] which has been published
under the editorship of Andrei Kraevsky[12] so that she'll
be able to talk about all subjects. Most of all have her
read the progressive political analysts of the *St. Petersburg News*, checking daily with *The Hair*. I suppose that
the owner will agree to bring me, together with the
crocodile, to my wife's brilliant salon. I shall stand in
the box in the center of our magnificent drawing room
and I shall spout witticisms which I will have culled
that same morning. To a gentleman of state I shall communicate my projects; with the poet I shall speak in
rhymes; with the ladies I shall be amusing and ador-
ingly moral, inasmuch as I pose no danger whatsoever
for their husbands. For all the rest I shall serve as an
example of submissiveness to fate and the will of providence. I shall make my wife a glittering literary lady; I
shall promote her and interpret her for the public. As
my wife, she must be full of the grandest virtues, and
if Andrei Aleksandrovich [Kraevsky] is justly named
our Russian Alfred de Musset, then with even greater
justness will she be named our Russian Yevgeniya
Tur."[13]

I must confess that this entire nonsense was somewhat typical of our usual Ivan Matveich, but nevertheless it still occurred to me that he was now in a delirium
and raving. It was that selfsame, everyday Ivan Matveich,

but observed through a lense that magnified twenty-fold.

"My friend," I asked him, "are you relying on longevity? And, in general, do tell me: are you well? How do you eat, how do you sleep, how do you breathe? I am your friend and you must agree that the incident is all too supernatural. Consequently, my curiosity is all too natural."

"Idle curiosity and nothing more," he replied sententiously. "But you will have your satisfaction. You ask how I've settled down in the bowels of the monster? First of all, to my amazement, the crocodile has turned out to be completely empty. Its interior consists of what seems to be an enormous empty bag made of rubber, something like the manufactured rubber goods that are prevalent here on Gorokhovaya Street, Morskaya Street, and, if I am not mistaken, on Vosnesensky Prospect. Otherwise, do you imagine that I could find room inside it?"

"Is it possible?" I cried in plain amazement. "Can a crocodile be completely empty?"

"Completely," Ivan Matveich insisted with authority. "And, in all probability, the crocodile has been so constructed in accordance with the laws of nature itself. A crocodile possesses only jaws, equipped with sharp teeth, and in addition to the jaws, a significantly long tail. Properly speaking, that is all there is to it. In the middle between these two extremities is situated an empty space enclosed by something in the form of rubber, most likely of all by rubber."

"What about the ribs, the stomach, the intestines, the liver, the heart?" I interrupted him almost angrily.

"Nothing, absolutely nothing of the sort, and probably there never was. All of that is the idle fantasy of frivolous travellers. Just as people inflate hemorrhoidal cushions, I am now inflating the crocodile with myself. It is unbelievably elastic. Room could be made for you here beside me, as a family friend, if you possessed the magnanimity, and still there would be room even with you present. As a last resort I am even thinking of instructing Yelena Ivanovna to join me here. Incidentally, this vacuous structure of the crocodile is in complete accord with the laws of the natural sciences. Let us suppose, for example, that you are to construct a new crocodile. Naturally, the question occurs to you: what is the fundamental characteristic of a crocodile? The answer is clear: to swallow people. How are we to realize the construction of a crocodile so that it can swallow people? This answer is even clearer: by constructing it empty. It has long been established by physics that nature abhors a vacuum. In keeping with this, the inside of a crocodile must therefore be empty so as not to endure a vacuum, and, consequently, so that it can ceaselessly swallow and fill itself up with everything that comes to hand. And that is the sole logical reason why all crocodiles swallow our brethren. This is not the case in the structure of a human being: the emptier the human head, for example, the less it senses the need to fill itself, and that is the one exception to the general rule. All of this is as clear to me now as day. I have perceived all of this with my own intellect and experience, finding myself, so to speak, in the bowels of nature, in its retort, hearkening to the beating of its pulse. Even etymology agrees with me, because the name itself of the crocodile designates voraciousness. Crocodile, *Crocodillo*, is obviously an Italian word, taken, perhaps, from the ancient Egyptian pharaohs, and, obviously, coming from the French root *croquer* which means 'to eat', 'to have a snack', and generally to use for food. I intend to expound all of this in the form of an initial lecture to the public who will gather at Yelena Ivanovna's salon when I am brought there in the box."

"My friend, shouldn't you perhaps at least take a purgative now!" I cried involuntarily. ("He has a temperature, he's in fever!" I repeated in horror under my breath.)

"Nonsense!" He replied scornfully. "And what is more, that would be quite inconvenient in my present situation. Incidentally, I had some idea that you would bring up the topic of a purgative."

"My friend, but how . . . how are you able to take food now? Have you eaten today or not?"

"No, but I am not hungry, and now most likely I shall never again take food. And that too is completely understandable: filling the entire inside of the crocodile with myself, I have made it satisfied for good. Now it won't be necessary to feed it for several years. On the other hand, since it has been made satisfied with me, it will naturally pass on to me all the life fluids from its body. This is reminiscent of some of those refined coquettes who cover themselves and all their bodies at night with raw cutlets and then, after taking their morning bath, become fresh, supple, juicy and seductive. In this fashion, as I nourish the crocodile with myself, I, in turn, receive sustenance from it. Consequently, we are feeding each other in a reciprocal fashion. But since it is difficult even for a crocodile to digest a person like me, then, naturally, it must sense a certain heaviness in its stomach while attempting to do so—a feeling which, by the way, I do not share. This is why, in order not to cause any unnecessary pain to the monster I rarely turn from side to side. Although I could turn about, out of humaneness I do not do so. This is the only shortcoming in my present position. In an allegorical sense Timofei Semyonich is right in saying that I am a layabout. But I shall prove that even while being a layabout it is possible to revolutionize the fate of mankind. All the great ideas and trends of our newspapers and journals are obviously being produced by layabouts. That is why their ideas are called armchair ideas, but who gives a straw that they are so called! I shall now invent an entire social system and you will not believe how easy it is! All you have to do is isolate yourself off in a corner or even end up inside a crocodile, close your eyes and immediately you will invent an entire paradise for all of mankind. Just a while ago, after you left, I immediately set to work inventing and I've already invented three systems and now I am devising a fourth. True, at first everything must be refuted. But it's so easy to refute from within a crocodile. Moreover, it all seems to be much clearer from inside a crocodile . . . Incidentally, there are other shortcomings in my position, albeit minor ones. It is somewhat damp inside a crocodile and it seems to be covered with slime. What's more, it still smells somewhat of rubber, precisely the way my rubber galoshes from last year do. That's all of it, there are no other shortcomings."

"Ivan Matveich," I interrupted, "These are all marvels that I can barely believe. And do you really intend to go your entire life without eating?"

"What kind of nonsense are you worrying about, you of a carefree, idle mind! I'm speaking to you about lofty ideas, whereas you . . . Try to comprehend that now I am sated simply by those lofty ideas which have illumined the night which surrounds me. Incidentally, after talking it over with his most generous mother, both the kindhearted owner and she have decided between themselves that every morning they will insert into the jaws of the crocodile a bent metallic tube something like a pipe through which I might draw in coffee or bouillon with white bread soaked in it. The pipe has already been ordered in the neighborhood, but I suppose that this is a superfluous luxury. I hope to live for at least a thousand years if it is true that crocodiles live that long—and now that I've thought about it, have a look tomorrow in some book on natural history and inform me, because I might be mistaken, having confused the crocodile with some other fossil. There is only one consideration that disturbs me somewhat: since I am dressed in cloth and I am wearing boots, then obviously the crocodile cannot digest me. What is more, I am alive and therefore will resist being digested with all of my will, for, understandably, I do not want to be turned into what all food is turned into, since that would be too humiliating for me. But there is one thing I fear: over a period of a thousand years the cloth of my jacket, which unfortunately is of Russian manufacture, can decay, and then, finding myself without clothing and all my indignation to the contrary, I most likely will begin to be digested. Although in the daytime I shall not allow that to happen under any circumstances, nevertheless at night, while asleep, when will power departs from a person, I could be overtaken by the most humiliating fate of any old potato, pancake or piece of veal. That kind of idea plunges me into a fury. For that reason alone the tariff ought to be changed and incentives given to the importation of English cloth which is stronger, and, consequently, will resist nature longer in the event that one ends up in a crocodile. I shall communicate my idea at the first opportunity to one of the gentlemen of state, and at the same time to the political analysts on our Petersburg daily newspapers. Let them raise a cry. I hope that this will not be the only thing they adopt from me now. I foresee that every morning an entire mob of them, armed with their editorial quarter-roubles, will crowd around me in order to seize on my thoughts regarding the telegrams received the day before. In short, I imagine my future in the rosiest of hues."

("Delirium, delirium!" I whispered to myself.)

"My friend, what about freedom?" I declared, wishing to have his opinion in full. "After all, you are, so to speak, in a dungeon and how is a person supposed to enjoy freedom then?"

"You are foolish," he replied. "Uncivilized people

love independence, whereas wise people love order, but there is no order . . ."[14]

"Ivan Matveich, have mercy, for goodness' sake!"

"Quiet and listen!" He shrieked in vexation that I had interrupted him. "Never before have I soared in spirit as now. In my cramped asylum there is one thing that I fear: the literary criticism of the thick journals and the jeers of our satirical newspapers. I fear that the frivolous, the foolish, the envious and, in general, the nihilists, will hold me up to mockery. But I shall take measures. I am waiting impatiently for the public's reactions tomorrow, and, especially, the opinions of the newspapers. Inform me about the newspapers tomorrow."

"Fine, tomorrow I'll bring an entire pile of newspapers."

"Tomorrow will still be too early to expect the newspaper reactions because the notices are printed only on the fourth day. But from today on come every evening by way of the inside entrance from the courtyard. I intend to use you as my secretary. You will read the newspapers and magazines to me and I shall dictate my thoughts to you and give you instructions. In particular don't forget the telegrams. Make sure that all the European telegrams are here every day. But enough. Probably you want to sleep now. Off you go home and don't think about what I just said about criticism. I am not afraid of it, because it is in a critical situation itself. All you have to do is be wise and virtuous and you will be put on a pedestal without fail. If not Socrates, then Diogenes, or the two of them together—that will be my future role in humanity."

Ivan Matveich hastened to express himself to me in this frivolous and obsessive fashion (true, he was delirious) just like those weak-willed old women about whom the proverb says that they cannot keep a secret. Moreover, everything he told me about the crocodile seemed highly suspect. How was it possible for a crocodile to be completely empty? I would wager that he had just been boasting out of conceit and partially in order to humiliate me. True, he was sick and a sick man had to be humored. But frankly I must admit that I could never stand Ivan Matveich. All my life, beginning right from childhood, I had wanted to and had been unable to escape his patronage. I had been on the verge of calling its quits with him a thousand times, but every time I was once again drawn to him as though I still went on hoping that I could prove something to him and have revenge for something. A strange thing was this friendship! I could positively say that I was friendly with him nine-tenths out of spite. However, this time we parted with emotion.

"Your friend, he is very clever man," the German said to me under his breath as he prepared to see me out. He had been diligently listening to our conversation all the while.

"*A propos*," I said, "so I won't forget, how much would you take for your crocodile in case someone thought of buying it from you?"

Hearing the question, Ivan Matveich waited with curiosity for the answer. It was apparent that he did not want the German to take a small amount; at least he gave a kind of peculiar grunt at my question.

At first the German would not even listen. He even grew angry. "No one dare buy my own crocodile!" he cried furiously and turned red like a boiled lobster. "I don't vant to sell crocodile. One million Taler I not take for crocodile. One hundred thirty Taler today I take from public, tomorrow ten thousand Taler I taking, and then one hundred thousand Taler every day I taking. To sell I don't vant!"

Ivan Matveich even started to chuckle with pleasure.

Plucking up my courage, coldbloodedly and logically, for I was fulfilling the responsiblity of a true friend, I pointed out to the unbridled German that his calculations were not quite correct; that if every day he collected a hundred thousand, then at the end of four days all of Petersburg would have come calling and then no one would be left from whom to collect; that life and death was in God's hands; that the crocodile could somehow split open; whereas Ivan Matveich might fall ill and die; etc., etc.

The German grew thoughtful.

"Him vill I give drops from pharmacy," he said, having given it thought, "and your friend not going to die."

"What good are drops?" I said. "But bear in mind that a legal trial might be initiated. The spouse of Ivan Matveich might demand her legal husband. Here you are intending to get rich, but do you intend to set aside at least some kind of pension for Yelena Ivanovna?"

"No, I vill not intend!" The German replied sternly and resolutely.

"No, I vill not intend!" The mother repeated almost spitefully.

"So, wouldn't it be better for you to take something now, all at once, even though it's moderate, yet certain and reliable, rather than abandoning yourself to the unknown? I consider it my duty to add that I am not asking merely out of idle curiosity."

The German took his mother and went off for consultations with her into the corner where the cage with the largest and most hideous of all the collections of monkeys stood.

"Now you'll see!" Ivan Matveich said to me.

As far as I was concerned, at that moment I was consumed with the desire, first of all, to give the German a painful thrashing, and secondly, to give the mother an even more painful thrashing, and thirdly, to give Ivan Matveich the biggest and most painful thrashing of all because of his unbridled vanity. But all of that paled in significance when compared with the greedy German's response.

Having consulted with his mother, he demanded, in return for his crocodile, fifty thousand roubles worth of lottery tickets, a stone house on Gorokhovskaya Street with his own apothecary's shop attached to it, and, in addition, the rank of a Russian colonel.

"You see!" Ivan Matveich cried triumphantly. "I told you! Except for the last insane wish to be promoted to a colonel, he is completely right, because he fully understands the present value of the monster which he is showing. The principle of economics comes first!"

"For goodness' sake!" I started to shout furiously at the German, "What do you want to be a colonel for? What feat have you performed, what service have you rendered, what military fame have you achieved? Well, are you not insane after all?"

"You insane!" The insulted German cried. "No, I very smart man, but you very stoopid! I earn colonel, because I show crocodile and live Russian *Hofrat*, he vas sitting inside, but Russian do not show crocodile and live Russian *Hofrat* he vas sitting inside! I am very smart man und I vant very much being colonel!"

"Farewell, then, Ivan Matveich!" I shouted, trembling with fury and I practically ran out of the crocodile room. I felt that one minute more and I would not be able to answer for myself. The unnatural expectations of these two dolts were unbearable. The cold air refreshed me and moderated my indignation somewhat. Finally, spitting energetically up to fifteen times in both directions, I took a cab, arrived home, undressed and flung myself into bed. More vexing than anything was the fact that I had ended up being his secretary. So go ahead now and perish from boredom there every evening, carrying out the responsiblity of a true friend! I was ready to pummel myself for that, and in fact, after I had extinguished the candle and pulled the blanket over myself, I struck myself several times on the head and other parts of the body with my fist. That calmed me somewhat and I finally fell into what was even a very deep sleep, because I was very tired. All night long I kept dreaming of nothing but monkeys, but towards morning I had a dream about Yelena Ivanovna . . .

CHAPTER IV

It is my conjecture that I dreamt about the monkeys because they were locked up in the cage at the crocodile owners, but Yelena Ivanovna constituted another matter.

I shall say right away that I loved this woman. But I hasten—with the utmost speed—I hasten to make a qualification: I loved her as a father, neither more nor less. I make this conclusion because on many occasions I felt an irresistible desire to kiss her on the head or on her sweet little rosy cheek. And although I never actually did so, nevertheless I do confess that I would not have refused to kiss her even on the lips. And not just on the lips, but on her teeth which always stood out so delightfully, just like a row of attractive, select pearls when she laughed. And she did laugh with amazing frequency. On tender occasions Ivan Matveich would call her his "sweet bit of nonsense"—a name that was extraordinarily appropriate and justified. She was a confection of a lady and nothing more. This is why I cannot comprehend in the least why that very same Ivan Matveich took it into his head to imagine our Russian Yevgeniya Tur in his spouse. In any case, my dream, if one were to ignore the monkeys, made the most pleasant impression on me, and, as I mentally went over all the events of the preceding day while taking my morning tea, I decided to drop in on Yelena Ivanovna at once on my way to work, which, incidentally, I was obliged to do by virtue of being a friend of the family.

In a tiny little room leading into the bedroom, in their so-called small salon—although their large salon was also small—on a small, decorative, little sofa, sitting at a small little tea table, wearing a diaphanous morning negligee, was Yelena Ivanovna and she was drinking her coffee out of a tiny little cup into which she kept dipping toasted bread. She was seductively attractive, yet seemed to me somehow pensive at the same time.

"Ah, so it's you, you naughty man!" She greeted me with a distracted smile. "Sit down, you frivolous creature, have some coffee. Well, what were you doing yesterday? Did you go to the masquerade?"

"Did you really go? I wasn't about to go . . . moreover, I was visiting our prisoner yesterday . . ."

I sighed and as I accepted the coffee I assumed a pious expression.

"Who? What prisoner is that? Ah, yes! The poor soul! Well, how is he, bored? By the way . . . I wanted to ask you . . . Could I ask for a divorce now?"

"A divorce!" I cried with indignation and almost spilled the coffee. ("It's that fellow with the dark complexion!" I thought to myself in a fury.)

There was a dark fellow with a moustache, working in the construction department, who came visiting them far too often and was extremely successful at amusing Yelena Ivanovna. I must admit that I hated him and there was no doubt that he had already managed to see Yelena Ivanovna yesterday either at the masquerade, or, most likely, right here, and say all manner of nonsense to her!

"But really," Yelena Ivanovna said hastily, just as though she had been prompted, "if he's going to sit in the crocodile and probably not return for his whole life, am I supposed to wait for him! A husband is supposed to live at home and not inside a crocodile . . ."

"But, after all, no one could have foreseen this event," I was on the point of saying in extreme agitation.

"Ah, no, don't speak, don't, don't!" She cried, suddenly quite angered. "You've always been so repulsive to me, such a good-for-nothing! There's nothing to be done with you, you can't give any advice! Strangers have already been telling me that I would be given a divorce because Ivan Matveich won't receive any salary now."

"Yelena Ivanovna! Is this you I hear?" I cried pathetically. "What malefactor could have put you up to this! And a divorce on such nonexistent grounds as salary is totally impossible. And poor, poor Ivan Matveich, so to speak, is entirely consumed with love for you, even inside the bowels of the monster. Moreover, he's melting from love, like a lump of sugar. Only just yesterday evening, while you were having a good time at the masquerade, he mentioned that as a last resort perhaps he would decide to summon you, as his legal spouse, to join him inside the bowels of the crocodile, all the more so because the the crocodile turns out to be extremely spacious not only for two people, but even for three . . ."

At this point I hastened to tell her this entire interesting portion of my conversation the evening before with Ivan Matveich.

"What, what!" She shouted in amazement. "You want me to crawl in there to join Ivan Matveich? That's a good one! And how am I supposed to crawl in there, wearing a hat and my crinolines? Lord, what stupidity! What a fine sight I'll make crawling in there and someone most likely will see me doing it . . . That's ridiculous! And what am I supposed to eat there? . . and . . . and how will I do . . . when I . . . ah, my Lord, what have they concocted? . . And what amusements are there? . . You say that it smells of rubber there? And what if he and I have an argument, am I supposed to just lie beside him anyway? Ugh, how repulsive!"

"I agree, I agree with all your arguments, dearest Yelena Ivanovna," I interrupted, trying to express myself with the understandable enthusiasm of a person when he feels that right is on his side. "But there is one thing which you haven't appreciated in all of this. You have not appreciated the fact that if he sends for you, it means that he cannot live without you. It means that it's a question of love, a love that is passionate, faithful and longing . . . You have not appreciated love, dear Yelena Ivanovna, love, I say!"

"No, no, I don't want to hear anything!" She kept waving me off with her small, attractive hand on which the pink nails that had just been washed and cleaned with a brush were gleaming. "You're repulsive! You will drive me to tears. Crawl inside there yourself if that will please you. After all, you're the friend, so go ahead and lie down there beside him for the sake of friendship and argue with him all your life about some boring sciences or other . . ."

"You are mocking this proposition unjustly," I interrupted the frivolous woman pompously. "Ivan Matveich was asking me to go anyway. Of course, it's duty that draws you there, whereas for me it is magnanimity alone. But when he was telling me yesterday about the extraordinary elasticity of the crocodile, Ivan Matveich alluded quite clearly to the fact that there was room not only for the two of you, but for me too, as a friend of the family, for the three of us together, particularly if I wanted to, and for that reason . . ."

"You mean, the three of us?" Yelena Ivanovna cried, staring at me in amazement. "So you mean that we, all three of us, will be there together? Ha-ha-ha! How stupid the two of you are! Ha-ha-ha! I'll be pinching you there all the while, without fail, what a good-for-nothing you are, ha-ha-ha! Ha-ha-ha!"

Throwing herself against the back of the sofa, she roared with laughter until the sweet little tears came. All of this—both the tears and the laughter—was so seductive that I could bear it no longer and rushed to cover her hands with ardent kisses and she did not resist although she tweaked me lightly on the ears as a sign of reconciliation.

Thereupon we both cheered up and I told her in detail all of Ivan Matveich's plans from the day before. She was very pleased by the thought of the evening receptions and a salon open to the public.

"The only thing is that I'll need a lot of new dresses," she remarked. "Therefore, Ivan Matveich must send as much of his salary as quickly as possible . . . Only . . . only really," she added pensively, "will they really bring him here in a box? That's quite absurd. I don't want my husband to be carried in a box. I shall be very ashamed in front of the guests . . . No, no, I don't want that."

"Incidentally, before I forget, did Timofei Semyonich visit you yesterday evening?"

"Ah, he did. He came to console me, and just imagine, we spent the whole time playing trump cards. He was playing for sweets and if I lost he would kiss my hands. Such a good-for-nothing and, imagine, he almost went to the masquerade with me. Truly!"

"He was infatuated!" I remarked. "And who wouldn't be infatuated with you, you seductive lady!"

"Now that's enough, off with you and your compliments! Wait, I'll give you a pinch for the road. I've learned terribly well how to pinch now. Well, how do you like that! By the way, did you say that Ivan Matveich was talking a great deal about me yesterday?"

"Hm-m, no, not that much, actually . . . I must confess to you that he was thinking more about the fate of all mankind and wanted . . ."

"Well, never mind him! Don't bother! Really, it's terribly boring. I'll visit him somehow. I shall go tomorrow without fail. Only not today. I have a headache, and, besides, there'll be so many people there . . . They'll say: 'That's his wife.' They'll shame me . . . Farewell. Will you . . . be there in the evening?"

"With him? Yes, yes, I will. He told me to come and bring the newspapers."

"Well, that's marvellous. Now off you go and read to him. But don't call on me this evening. I'm not well, or maybe I'll be visiting. Well, farewell, you naughty man."

("It's the dark fellow who'll be with her this evening," I thought to myself.)

Naturally, at the office I did not let it show that I was being devoured by such worries and cares. But I soon remarked that some of our more progressive newspapers were being passed from hand to hand among my colleagues with somewhat unusual speed and were being read with extremely serious expressions. The first one that came into my hands was *The Tabloid*,[15] a kind of newspaper without any particular tendency, merely humanitarian in general, for which it was by and large despised in our country, even though people read it. It was with some amazement that I read the following in it:

"Yesterday, in our vast capital, which is adorned with magnificent buildings, extraordinary rumors were circulating. A certain Mr. X, who is a well-known society gastronome, probably jaded by Borelle's[16] cuisine and the . . . club, entered the building of *The Arcade*, at the spot where an enormous crocodile, which had just been brought to the capital, was on display, and demanded that the crocodile be prepared for his dinner. Having struck a bargain with the owner, he immediately set about devouring him (not the owner, that is, who is an exceptionally mild German with a tendency to preciseness, but his crocodile) while still alive, slicing off juicy pieces with his penknife and swallowing them with extreme haste. Little by little the entire crocodile disappeared into his corpulent innards so that he was even about to set about the mongoose, the crocodile's constant companion, probably thinking that the latter would be just as tasty. We are not in the least opposed to this new product which has long been familiar to foreign gastronomes. We have even been predicting this beforehand. In Egypt English lords and travellers are catching crocodiles by the masses and are using the spinal hump of the monster in the form of beef steaks, with mustard, onion and potatoes. The French, who arrived with Lesseps,[17] prefer the paws, baked in hot embers, something, incidentally, which they do in order to spite the English who make fun of them. Probably in our country we value both the one and the other. For our part, we are happy at the new branch of industry which by and large is lacking in our powerful and diverse fatherland. Following this first crocodile, which has disappeared in the innards of the Petersburg gastronome, a year will probably not go by before they are imported here by the hundreds. And why should the crocodile not be acclimatized to Russia? If the

water of the Neva is too cold for these interesting foreigners, then there are ponds in the capital and rivers
and lakes outside the city. Why not, for example, raise
the crocodiles in Pargolovo or in Pavlovsk, in Moscow
right in the Presnensky Ponds and in the Samotyok?
While offering a pleasant and healthy fare for our
refined gastronomes, they could at the same time bring
pleasure to the ladies strolling by the ponds and give
the children instruction in natural history. From the
skins of crocodiles it would be possible to fashion boxes,
travelling bags, cigarette cases and purses, and, perhaps,
more than a few thousand roubles of Russian merchant
money in soiled bank notes, which are by and large
preferred by the merchantry, would be invested in
crocodile skin. We hope to return more than once to
this interesting subject."

Although I had had a premonition of something of
this nature, nevertheless, I was dismayed by the precipi-
tous speed of the news. Finding no one with whom I
could share my impressions, I turned to Prokhor Savvich who was sitting across from me and noticed that
he had been watching me for a long while and holding
the newspaper *The Hair* in his hands, as though prepar-
ing to pass it on to me. Silently he took the *Tabloid* from
me and as he handed *The Hair* over to me, he firmly
used his fingernail to underline the article which he
probably wanted to bring to my attention. This Prokhor
Savvich of ours was a very eccentric person. A taciturn
old bachelor, he never had anything to do with any of
us, spoke almost to no one at the office, always had his

own opinion about everything, but could not bear to inform anyone of it. He lived alone. Almost none of us had been in his apartment.

This is what I read in the place indicated in *The Hair*:

"Everyone knows that we are progressive and humane and wish to keep pace with Europe in this regard. But, despite all the attempts and efforts of our newspaper, we are far from having 'matured', as witnessed by the outrageous episode that occurred yesterday in *The Arcade* and which we have been predicting beforehand. A foreign proprietor arrived in the capital and brought with him a crocodile which he began to display to the public in *The Arcade*. We immediately hastened to greet this new branch of useful industry which generally has been lacking in our powerful and diverse fatherland. Then suddenly yesterday, at half-past five in the afternoon, a certain person of uncommon corpulence and in an inebriated state appeared in the store of the foreign proprietor, paid for admission and immediately, without any forewarning, crawled into the jaws of the crocodile, which, naturally, was obliged to swallow him, if for no other reason than out of a sense of self-preservation in order not to choke. Tumbling into the insides of the crocodile, the stranger immediately dozed off. Neither the cries of the foreign proprietor, nor the howling of his frightened family, nor even the threats to summon the police exerted any impression. From within the crocodile all that could be heard was laughter and a promise to use whipping rods (sic) to deal with the situation, whereas the wretched mammal, obliged to swallow such a mass, was streaming tears in vain. An uninvited guest is worse than a Tartar, but despite the proverb, the impudent visitor would not come out. We don't know how to explain barbaric facts like these which testify to our immaturity and tarnish us in the eyes of foreigners. The unbridled nature of the Russian character has found a worthy application for itself. The question is, what did this unbidden visitor want? A warm and comfortable lodging? But in the capital there are many beautiful houses with cheap and extremely comfortable apartments, with plumbing from the Nevsky, stairwells illuminated by gas and where not infrequently a doorman is hired by the owners. Let us further direct the attention of our readers to the very barbaric treatment of household pets: naturally it was difficult for the foreign crocodile to digest that kind of mass all at once and now it's lying there, inflated like a mountain and awaiting death in unbearable agony. For a long time now in Europe those who treat domestic pets inhumanely are prosecuted by the court. But despite our European enlightenment, our European sidewalks, our European construction of houses, we have not left our hallowed prejudices far behind: *The homes are new, yet the prejudices are old*[18]—and even the homes are not all that new, or at least the staircases. More than once in our newspaper we have mentioned that on the Petersburg side, in the home of the merchant Lukiyanov, the wooden stairwell steps have rotted, caved in and for a long while now have presented a danger for the soldier's wife, Afimiya Skapidarova who works for him and who is frequently obliged to climb the stairs with water or an armful of firewood. Finally our premonitions were justified: yesterday evening, at half past-nine in the evening, the soldier's wife, Afimiya Skapidarova, collapsed with a soup pot and broke her leg. We don't know whether Lukiyanov will repair his staircase now: a Russian is best at hindsight, but the sacrifice of this Russian, hopefully, has already been taken off to the hospital. This is precisely why we shall not tire of insisting that the street sweepers who clean the dirt from the wooden sidewalks on Vyborgskaya should not dirty the feet of passers-by, but should put the dust in piles as they do in Europe in order to keep our boots clean . . . etc., etc."

"What is this?" I said, looking in some bewilderment at Prokhor Savvich. "What's this all about?"

"What do you mean?"

"For goodness' sake, rather than feeling sorry for Ivan Matveich, they feel sorry for the crocodile."

"What do you expect? It's a creature, a mammal, that's what they feel sorry for. Are we different from Europe? There they feel very sorry for crocodiles. He-he-he!"

Having said that, the eccentric Prokhor Savvich stuck his nose into his papers and did not speak a single word more.

I hid *The Hair* and *The News* in my pocket and, in addition, collected as many old copies of *The News* and *The Hair* as I could find, and although evening was still a long way off, this time I slipped out of the office somewhat earlier in order to visit *The Arcade* and at least observe from a distance what was going on there and eavesdrop on the various opinions and trends. I had the premonition that there would be a great crush and in any event I buried my face more deeply in the collar of my coat because I felt a little ashamed for some reason— unaccustomed to publicity as we were. But I feel that I do not have a right to pass on my own prosaic feelings in view of such a remarkable and original event.

NOTES

1. The actual Russian subtitle, "Passazh v passazhe," is a
   (scatological?) pun. *The Passage* (rendered in this translation as *The Arcade*) represented a popular form of commercial architecture imported from Europe in the second half
   of the nineteenth century. The construction usually consisted of a closed gallery with commercial shops along
   either side and exiting on to parallel streets. Moscow's
   State Department Store, *GUM*, would be a good contemporary example. The same word in Russian also signifies
   an unexpected occurence or surprising twist of events.
   David Magarshack's rendition of the subtitle as "An
   Amusing Event at the Amusement Arcade" might appeal
   to some readers. The subtitle appears to have been inspired
   by an article Dostoevsky was writing when the idea of the
   story for "The Crocodile" occurred to him. That article
   was entitled "Puns in Life and Literature" ("Kalambury v
   zhizni i literature", *Epokha*, 10, 1864) and represented a

humorous diatribe directed against A. A. Kraevsky and others. In particular, Dostoevsky attacked the pliant liberal and European attitudes of the Russian press that were determined more by "commercial" than philosophical reasons. Kraevsky was taken to task because he was apparently trying to downgrade the literary importance of Russia's "thick journals" in favor of the dailies—despite the fact that he was a publisher-editor of both types. The contradictory position of Kraevsky was used by Dostoevsky to develop an amusing but withering series of puns to expose Kraevsky's duplicity.

2. Dostoevsky's epigram apparently had its origins in an obscure and nonsensical greeting that enjoyed great popularity on the streets of Paris in the 1840's.

3. Lavrov, Pyotr Lavrovich (1823-1900). Russian scholar, critic and thinker. One of the founders and theoreticians of revolutionary populism and among the first to study Marx in Russia. He was considered a materialist, positivist and follower of Chernyshevsky. Gave a series of popular and controversial lectures in 1860 in the lecture hall of *The Arcade.*

4. Stepanov, Nikolai Aleksandrovich (1807-1877). Russian artist, cartoonist and editor / publisher of the satirical journals *The Spark* (*Iskra*) and *Alarum* (*Budil'nik*) which belonged to the "democratic press".

5. Dostoevsky intended a pun with ironic political overtones here. The word in Russian is *vsporot'* which can mean either "to whip" or to "rip open".

6. *The Petersburg News* (*Peterburgskie izvestiya*) and *The Hair* (*Volos*) are satirical references to two publications owned

by A. A. Kraevsky: *The Petersburg Record (Peterburgskie vedomosti)* and *The Voice (Golos)*. See note 12 on Kraevsky.

7. Originally only members of the gentry or aristocracy were allowed to hold bureaucratic posts. This privilege was extended to children of humbler origins who had received their education in schools that were attached to army installations.

8. *Son of the Fatherland (Syn otechestva)*. A Russian historical, political and literary periodical founded in 1812. Up until the Decembrist revolt in 1825 it was a moderately progressive publication that included the writings of a number of the Russian Decembrists. After 1825 it became exceedingly conservative and monarchist under the editorship of N. I. Grech and F. V. Bulgarin who were regarded with suspicion by Russia's progressive writers because of their purported ties with the secret police. Beginning in 1862 it appeared as a daily newspaper after various intermediate stages as a monthly, bi-monthly and weekly publication.

9. Fourier, Charles (1772-1837). A French utopian socialist whose ideas were popular during the 1860's in the Russian democratic press.

10. Garnier-Pagès, Louis Antoine (1803-1878). A French political figure who participated in the revolutions of 1830 and 1848. Author of *Histoire de la Révolution de 1848*. From 1864 he occupied various judicial and legislative posts.

11. A reference to the *Encyclopaedic Dictionary (Entsiklopedicheskiy slovar')* compiled by Russian scholars and writers. The first volume appeared in 1861 under the editorship of A. A. Kraevsky and caused a minor scandal in more sophisticated literary circles because Kraevsky was thought to be

incompetent and merely seeking self-aggrandizement. Dostoevsky was among those who shared such opinions. P. L. Lavrov became the editor for the subsequent volumes. The publication ceased in 1863 with volume six.

12. Kraevsky, Andrei Aleksandrovich (1810-1889). A famous Russian publisher and journalist. At one point or another during his extraordinary life, Kraevsky was the publisher or editor of some of Russia's most prestigious literary journals and newspapers, including Pushkin's *The Contemporary* (*Sovremennik*), *The Literary Gazette* (*Literaturnaya gazeta*), *The Russian Pensioner* (*Russkiy invalid*), *The Petersburg Record* (*S-Peterburgskie vedomosti*), *The Voice* (*Golos*). From 1839 he published *Notes of the Fatherland* (*Otechestvennye zapiski*) wherein the works of Lermontov, Belinsky, Turgenev, Herzen, Dostoevsky *et al.* were printed. Kraevsky vascillated between the conservative-reactionary and liberal camps, depending upon the political climate. Particularly in the later 1850's and throughout the 1860's he supported a moderate form of bourgeois European liberalism and progressivism. He had a reputation for being a literary and political opportunist and was known to exploit his writers and journalists. His *Petersburg Record* and *The Voice* were two of the most commercially successful publications of the 1860's.

13. Tur, Yevgeniya (pseud. of Yelizaveta Vasilyevna Salias-de-Turnemir, 1815-1892). Russian writer, critic and sister of the famous playwright, A. V. Sukhovo-Kobylin. Her works were well regarded by Turgenev and others, but did not enjoy great popularity with readers. In the 1850's and 1860's she was a prominent literary critic on a number of leading Russian journals.

14. This is a slightly altered quotation from N. M. Karamzin's *Marfa Posadnitsa* (1802). The entire quotation should read: "Uncivilized peoples love independence, whereas wise peoples love order; but there is no order without autocratic authority."

15. This is a reference to *The Petersburg Tabloid. A Newspaper of City Life and Literature* (*Peterburgskiy listok. Gazeta gorodskoy zhizni i literatury*). Founded in 1864 as a daily.

16. Borelle was the owner of an expensive restaurant in Petersburg that was famous for its exotic cuisine.

17. Lesseps, Ferdinand Marie, Vicomte de (1805-1894). French engineer and diplomat who headed the project for the Suez Canal.

18. A quotation from Griboedov's play, *Woe from Wit* (*Gore ot uma*, II, 4).

APPENDIX

SOMETHING PERSONAL

I have been urged on a number of occasions to write my literary memoirs. I don't know whether I will and, besides, I have a poor memory. What's more, it makes me sad to remember; in general I don't like to remember. But several episodes from my literary career involuntarily come to mind with extreme clarity despite my poor memory. Here is an example of one story.

This excerpt is taken from Dostoevsky's *Diary of a Writer* (*Dnevnik pisatelya*), as published in F. M. Dostoevskii, *Polnoe sobranie sochinenii* (Leningrad, 1980), XX, 23-31.

One spring morning I dropped in on the now-deceased Yegor Petrovich Kovalevsky. He very much liked my novel *Crime and Punishment* which appeared at that time in *The Russian Herald*. He praised it enthusiastically and passed on what for me was a very precious criticism from a certain person whose name I cannot produce. Meanwhile, two publishers of two different journals entered the room one after the other. One of these journals subsequently acquired a number of subscribers that was unprecedented for one of our monthly publications, but at that time it was just getting started. The other, however, was already in the process of ending an existence that had been both remarkable and influential for the public; but at the time, on that particular morning, its publisher still had no idea that his publication was already reaching the end of the line. It was with this latter publisher that I went off into another room where we found ourselves alone . . .

"Well, we gave you a good thrashing," he said to me (meaning for *Crime and Punishment* in his journal).

"I know," I said.

"But do you know why?"

"On principle, most likely."

"Because of Chernyshevsky."

I was stunned with amazement:

"Mr. X, who wrote the critical article," the publisher continued, "explained it to me like this: 'His novel is good, but because two years ago he was not ashamed to insult an unfortunate exile and make a caricature out of him in his novella, I'll give his novel a thrashing.'"

"So it's still that same stupid gossip over 'The Crocodile?'" I cried, realizing what it was about. "But do you really believe that too? Have you read 'The Crocodile' yourself?"

"No, I haven't."

"But it's all gossip, the most vile gossip imaginable. One would have to have the mind and poetic instinct of a Bulgarin to read some 'civic' allegory, and what's more, on Chernyshevsky, into this mere trifle, this comic tale! If you knew how stupid this exaggerated business is. I'll never forgive myself for the fact that I didn't protest against this foul libel as soon as it was spread two years ago!"

This conversation of mine with the publisher whose journal has long since perished took place about seven years ago and to this day I haven't protested against the "libel"—whether for reasons of neglect or simply because "there wasn't time". Meanwhile, this foul act which has been ascribed to me remained in the minds of other persons as an indisputable fact, gained headway in literary circles, even reached the general public and on more than one occasion has been the source of unpleasantness for me. The time has come to say at least a few words about it, all the more so because now seems the opportune moment, and although you only have my word for it, nevertheless I will be refuting a libel that in itself is based on the words of others. By my long silence and neglect until now it might have seemed that I was merely confirming it.

The first time I met Nikolai Gavrilovich Chernyshevsky was in 1859, the very first year after returning from Siberia. I don't recall where or how it was. Afterwards we met several times, but not very frequently; we chatted, but not a great deal. Incidentally, we always shook hands. Herzen had said to me that Chernyshevsky had created an unpleasant impression on him, that is, with his appearance and manner. I liked Chernyshevsky's appearance and manner.

One morning on the door handle of my apartment I found one of the most remarkable proclamations that had appeared at the time; and there had been a great number of them then. It was entitled "To The Young Generation". It was impossible to imagine anything more absurd or stupid. Only some villain could have conceived of such outrageous contents and in such a ridiculous form so as to ruin both. I was terribly upset and melancholy all day. At the time it was all still so unprecedented and so close to home that it was difficult as of yet to completely fathom the motives of these people. It was difficult precisely for the reason that somehow one could not believe that mere nonsense underlay all the turmoil. I am not talking about the [political] movement as a whole at the time; I am talking only about the people. As far as the movement was concerned, that was a phenomenon that was grim, pathological, yet fateful, in its historical logic and one that will have its own serious page in the Petersburg period of our history. And the writing of that page is far from complete.

And because for a long time I had disagreed body and soul with both these people and the purpose of their movement, I suddenly grew annoyed and almost ashamed over their incompetence: "Why did they make it seem so stupid and incompetent?" And what did it have to do with me? But it wasn't their failure that caused me regret. In actual fact I didn't know a single one of the disseminators of the proclamations, nor do I know any of them to this day. But my melancholy stemmed from the fact that I failed to view this phenomenon as something that was atypical and merely a silly prank by precisely those kind of people that had nothing to do with me. I was depressed by one fact here: the level of education, of development and the minimal comprehension of reality depressed me terribly. Even though I had lived for three years in Petersburg and had witnessed other phenomena, I was somehow shocked by this proclamation on that morning and for me it appeared somehow as a new and surprising revelation: I had never surmised the existence of such triviality! It was precisely the degree of this triviality that frightened me. Towards evening I suddenly took it into my head to visit Chernyshevsky. Before then I had never once been at his home and had never thought of doing so any more than he had contemplated being at mine.

I remember that it was around five o'clock in the afternoon. I found Nikolai Gavrilovich all by himself, not a single servant was at home and he opened the door himself. He gave me an extremely warm greeting and took me into his study.

"Nikolai Gavrilovich, what's the meaning of this?" I pulled the proclamation out.

He took it as though it were something totally unfamiliar to him and read it. It consisted of no more than ten lines.

"What about it?" He asked me with a slight smile.

"Are they really that stupid and ridiculous? Is it not possible to curtail this villainy and put an end to it?"

His reply was quite sober and solemn:

"Do you really suppose that I sympathize with them and do you think that I could have taken part in the composition of this piece of paper?"

"Quite the contrary," I replied, "and I even consider it unnecessary to assure you of that. But in any event they must be stopped regardless. Your word bears weight with them and naturally they fear your opinion."

"I don't know any of them."

"I am certain of that. But it's not at all necessary to know them and speak with them personally. All you have to do is to declare your condemnation aloud anywhere and it will reach them."

"Perhaps it won't have any effect. Moreover, these phenomena are unavoidable as side effects."

"But nevertheless they are harmful to one and all."

At this point another guest rang, I don't recall who. I left. I consider it my duty to note that I spoke candidly with Chernyshevsky and I had the firm belief, even as I do now, that he did not "sympathize" with these disseminators. It seemed to me that Nikolai Gavrilovich was not displeased with my visit; a few days later he confirmed this by visiting me himself. He stayed more than an hour and I confess that I rarely had met a gentler and more cordial person, so that I was surprised at the time over critical remarks concerning his personality to the effect that he was harsh and unsociable. It became clear to me that he wanted to be friends with me and I recall that I was pleased by that. Later I was at his place once more and he at mine as well. Shortly thereafter I moved to Moscow for various reasons and lived there for about nine months. In this way our acquaintanceship, which had only just begun, was cut short. Then followed Chernyshevsky's arrest and exile. I was never able to find out anything about his case; nor do I know anything to this day.

About a year and a half later I had the idea of writing a fantastic tale somewhat in imitation of Gogol's "Nose". I had never before attempted to write in the fantastic genre. It was purely a literary prank, solely for comic effect. In fact I came up with several comic situations that I wanted to develop. Although it's not worth it, nevertheless I'll recount the plot so that one can understand what inferences were subsequently made . . . (*Dostoevsky now presents a lengthy and accurate description of the plot of "The Crocodile"*). That is the first part of this comic story. It isn't finished. Someday I'll finish it for certain although I had already forgotten about it and had to reread it to refresh my memory.

Now this is what people made of this insignificant piece of trivia. The story had barely appeared in the journal *Epoch* (1865) when' suddenly *The Voice* made a strange remark in a feuilleton. I don't recall it word for word and it's too long ago to look it up, but the sense was approximately the following: "It is said that the author of 'The Crocodile' has embarked upon this kind of path in vain; it will bring him neither honor nor anticipated profit", etc. etc. Then followed several of the most obscure and hostile barbs. I browsed through it, understood nothing and merely perceived that it contained a good deal of venom, but I didn't know why. Naturally, that obscure feuilletonistic review could not in itself do me any harm. None of the readers would have understood it any more than I did. But then suddenly a week later N. N. Strakhov said to me: "Do you know what they're thinking over there? Over there they're certain that your 'Crocodile' is an allegory, the story of Chernyshevsky's exile, and that you wanted to depict and ridicule Chernyshevsky." Even though I was amazed, I was not very upset. There's no end to the kind of conjectures people are likely to make! That particular opinion seemed to me too atypical and farfetched to gain impetus and I considered it completely unnecessary to protest. I shall never forgive myself for that, because that opinion did flourish and gain impetus. *Calomniez, il en restera toujours quelque chose.*

Incidentally, I am convinced even now that there was no reason for libel here at all: what was the reason, what was the purpose? I fought with practically no one in literature, at least not very seriously. Now, at this moment, I am speaking about myself for only the second time in a literary career of twenty-seven years. This was simply a matter of stupidity, a sullen, mistrustful stupidity that settled in someone's "tendentious" mind. I am convinced that this overactive mind is utterly certain to this very day that it was not mistaken and that I was indisputably mocking the unfortunate Chernyshevsky. I am even convinced that I could not change the view of that mind with whatever explanations and apologies that might be in my favor. But that's why this is such an overactive mind. (Of course, I am not speaking of Andrei Aleksandrovich [Kraevsky]; as the editor and publisher of his newspaper he has nothing to do with it, as is the usual case.)

What is the allegory about? Well, of course, the crocodile represents Siberia; the presumptuous and frivolous official is Chernyshevsky. He ends up in the crocodile and still nourishes the hope of lecturing the entire world. His weak-willed friend, whom he tyrannizes, represents Chernyshevsky's friends who are all still here. The attractive but silly wife of the official, who rejoices in her situation of "semi-widowhood", is . . . But at this point it becomes so foul that I don't want to dirty myself and continue the clarification of the allegory. (But meanwhile the allegory did flourish and it was perhaps precisely the latter allusion that flourished; I have indisputable proof of that.)

It means that people supposed that I, who myself was a former exile and convict, was exultant over the exile of another "unfortunate"; and, moreover, that I wrote a gleeful lampoon on the occasion. But where is the proof of that? In the allegory? But bring me whatever you wish . . . [Gogol's] "Notes of a Madman", [Derzhavin's] ode "To God", [Zagoskin's] *Yuriy Miloslavsky*, the verses of Fet—whatever you want—and I'll undertake to produce for you immediately, from the first ten lines chosen by you, that what we have here is an allegory about the Franco-Prussian War or a lampoon on the actor Gorbunov—in other words, on anyone you ask me to do so. Just recall how a long time ago, at the very end of the 1840's, for example, how the censors examined manuscripts and the see-through liners: there wasn't a line, there wasn't a dot in which they didn't suspect something, some kind of allegory. Better they produce something out of my entire life as proof that I look like a wicked, heartless lampooner and that such allegories might be expected of me.

It's precisely the haste and alacrity of such groundless inferences that bear witness, on the contrary, to a certain villainy of spirit of the accusers themselves, and to the vulgarity and inhumaneness of their view. Not even the very naivete of the conjecture can be excused in this case. Isn't that so? It's possible to be naively vile and nothing more.

Perhaps I despised Chernyshevsky personally? In order to forestall that accusation I intentionally related the earlier story about our brief and cordial acquaintance. People might say that it means nothing and that I nourished a secret hatred. But let them then produce the pretexts for this hatred if they have something to produce. There were none. On the other hand, I am convinced that Chernyshevsky himself would confirm the accuracy of my story of our meeting if someday he reads it. And God grant that he gets the opportunity to do so. I wish for that warmly and heartily, just as I sincerely sympathized and still sympathize with his misfortune.

But perhaps it was a case of hatred out of convictions?

But why? Chernyshevsky never offended me with

his convictions. One can have a great deal of respect for a person whose views differ radically from one's own. On this point, incidentally, I can offer something more than just my word and I even have some small proof. In one of the very last issues of the journal *Epoch* which was closing down at the time (possibly even the final one), there was a long critical article on Chernyshevsky's "famous" novel, *What Is To Be Done?* It was a remarkable article and came from a well-known pen. And what about it? All that was due to the mind and talent of Chernyshevsky was given in that article. There was even enthusiastic comment made on his novel. No one ever doubted his remarkable mind. Mere mention was made in our article about the peculiarities and deviations of that mind, but the very seriousness of the article bore witness to the appropriate respect that our critic possessed for the merits of the author under discussion. Now you must agree: if I had any hatred out of convictions, I would not, of course, have allowed an article in the journal where Chernyshevsky was spoken of with appropriate respect. And, indeed, I, and no one else, was the editor of *Epoch*.

Perhaps in printing the venomous allegory I was hoping to curry favor *en haut lieu*? But when and who might say of me that I seeking or profiting by some *lieu* in this sense, in other words, that I was selling my pen? I even believe that the author himself of the conjecture did not have that thought in mind despite all his naivete. Nor would it have flourished in the literary world if that was all the accusation consisted of.

APPENDIX

As far as the accusation is concerned that I was allegorically lampooning certain other domestic circumstances of Nikolai Gavrilovich, then once more I shall repeat that I do not even want to touch that point in my own "justification" in order not to dirty myself . . .

I am upset that I started to talk about myself on this occasion. This is what it means to write literary reminiscences. I shall never write them. I quite regret that I have undoubtedly bored the reader. But I am writing my diary, a diary that partially contains my personal impressions, and then quite recently a "literary" impression came to me which indirectly reminded me of this forgotten story about my forgotten "Crocodile".

[1873]

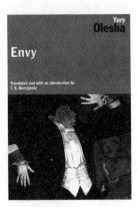